This igloo book belongs to:

Isabel

igloobooks

Published in 2019
by Igloo Books Ltd
Cottage Farm
Sywell
NN6 0BJ
www.igloobooks.com

GOL002 0319
10 12 13 11 9
ISBN: 978-0-85780-430-3

Printed and manufactured in China

Catch it,
Kitty

igloobooks

One morning, Kitty woke up and noticed a big, fluffy ball lying next to her basket. "I could have a lot of fun with this," she thought, bouncing over to have a closer look.

"This ball is very squishy," thought Kitty.
"It's perfect for jumping on."

Kitty rolled the ball to the sofa and climbed up onto the back. Just as she was about to jump on the ball, she heard Mousey, her friend, call, "Can I jump on it, too?"

"No!" said Kitty. "It's mine. I found it."

Kitty jumped right into the middle of the fluffy ball. What fun she was having! After a while, she noticed the ball was a little smaller.

Next, Kitty decided to bounce up and down on the fluffy ball.
"It's really springy!" said Kitty, bouncing higher and higher.

"That looks fun," said Puppy. "Can I play your bouncing game
with you, Kitty?" he asked. "No, you can't," replied Kitty.
"I found this ball and I'm going to bounce on it."

But by the time
Kitty had finished
the bouncing game,
the fluffy ball was
smaller still.

Then Kitty thought it would be fun to push the ball down the slide and let it splash in the puddle at the bottom. "That looks fun! Can we join in too, Kitty?" asked Hammy and Rabbit.

"No, you can't," said Kitty. "I found this ball and I'm going to push it down the slide.

"Weeeeee!" cried Kitty, following the ball down the slippery slide.

But by the time Kitty had finished the splashing game, the fluffy ball was even smaller.

Next, Kitty decided to play a catching game. She threw the fluffy ball high in the air and caught it. Then she did it again... and again.

When she stopped, the ball was even smaller still. After a while, Kitty grew bored. "It's no fun playing catch all by myself," she said. "It would be much nicer playing with all my friends."

So Kitty went to find them. "Will you play with me?" she
asked, shyly. "I'm sorry I didn't want to play catch with you."
"Of course we will!" they all cried, happily.
"Oh, thank you!" said Kitty. "I'm sorry I've been so mean."
"Don't worry," said Puppy, cheerfully.
"We can all play together now."

But by now, all that was left of the fluffy ball was a long piece of wool.

"Oh, dear. We can't play catch now," said Kitty, sadly.

"I know. Let's follow the wool and see where it leads us!"
cried Mousey.

Which is exactly what they did.

When they reached the end, they were amazed to see that the fluffy ball had turned into a big, fluffy blanket.

"What game can we play with a blanket," asked Kitty.
But nobody could think of anything.
Then Mousey piped up again.
"I've got an idea!" he said, excitedly. "We could
get under the blanket and play a great game of...

... hide-and-seek!"

"This is much better
than playing all on my own."
laughed Kitty.